ILLUMINATION PRESENTS

THE SECRET LIFE OF PETS

Adapted by David Lewman
Illustrated by Craig Kellman

 A GOLDEN BOOK · NEW YORK

universal
A COMCAST COMPANY

ILLUMINATION
ENTERTAINMENT

Hi! My name is Max. I'm the luckiest dog in the whole world. I live in New York City with my owner, Katie. She's the greatest! We have the perfect relationship. She'd do anything for me. And I'm her loyal protector.

Even when I make little mistakes, Katie understands that I'm not perfect, so she always forgives me. Our love is stronger than words . . . **or shoes**.

By the way, Katie has great taste in shoes. And her shoes taste great!

It's me and Katie. Katie and me. Us against the world.
No matter what comes our way. Together we can handle
whatever life throws at us. That's how it is, and that's
how we like it!

There's just one little problem with our relationship. Pretty much every day, Katie leaves. Sometimes I try stuff to get her to stay. I do all my best tricks.

I miss her so much while she's gone. All day, I sit by the front door of our apartment, waiting for her to come back.

Well, actually, I don't sit by the front door *all* day. Luckily, I have other friends who live in our apartment building and the building next door. They're pets like me. Most days they come to visit. We all miss our owners during the day, but at least we can keep each other company.

GIDGET is a Pomeranian. She lives in the building across the way. A Pomeranian looks like someone made a little dog out of puffballs. Every morning, Gidget jumps up onto a pillow in her window and calls across to me.

Gidget always asks me what my plans for the day are.
She thinks my life is very exciting. She must, because she
spends her whole day staring at me.

CHLOE the cat is always there for me when I need some good advice. She's real smart. All I have to do to visit her is go out our window and climb up the fire escape to the apartment Chloe lives in. Sometimes she comes down to my place.

But lately she's been having a little trouble squeezing through the window. You see, Chloe likes human food.

LOTS of human food. I think it must be a cat thing. As a dog, I stay focused on Katie coming home—but cats . . . cats do what cats do, I guess.

Sweetpea is a little bird called a budgie. But don't let his size fool you. His body may be small, but his imagination is big!

As soon as his owner leaves in the morning, Sweetpea likes to turn on a fan and a video of fighter jets zooming through a canyon . . .

. . . and then he flies right in front of the TV screen, pretending he's a fighter jet, too!

VROOOOM!

MEL is a pug. He's a big fan of pillows (for chewing), balls (for chasing), and delicious peanut butter (for eating). But there's one thing he definitely does not like at all—squirrels!

He thinks that squirrels are gonna try to take over the world.
I think he's wrong about that. But he is right about peanut butter.

LEONARD is a poodle. He lives in a fancy apartment. Looking at him, you might think he's kind of snobby, like his owner. But after his owner leaves for the day, telling him to be a good boy . . .

. . . Leonard pushes a button on the stereo with his nose to play loud, thumping, hard-rocking music! He and his friends shake their heads and shout along with the songs! Leonard definitely knows how to cut loose and **ROCK!**

BUDDY is a dachshund. He loves having his long body massaged. As soon as his owner heads out for the day, Buddy hurries into the kitchen. He jumps up on the counter, knocks the bowl off the mixer, and flips the switch.

WHIRRR!

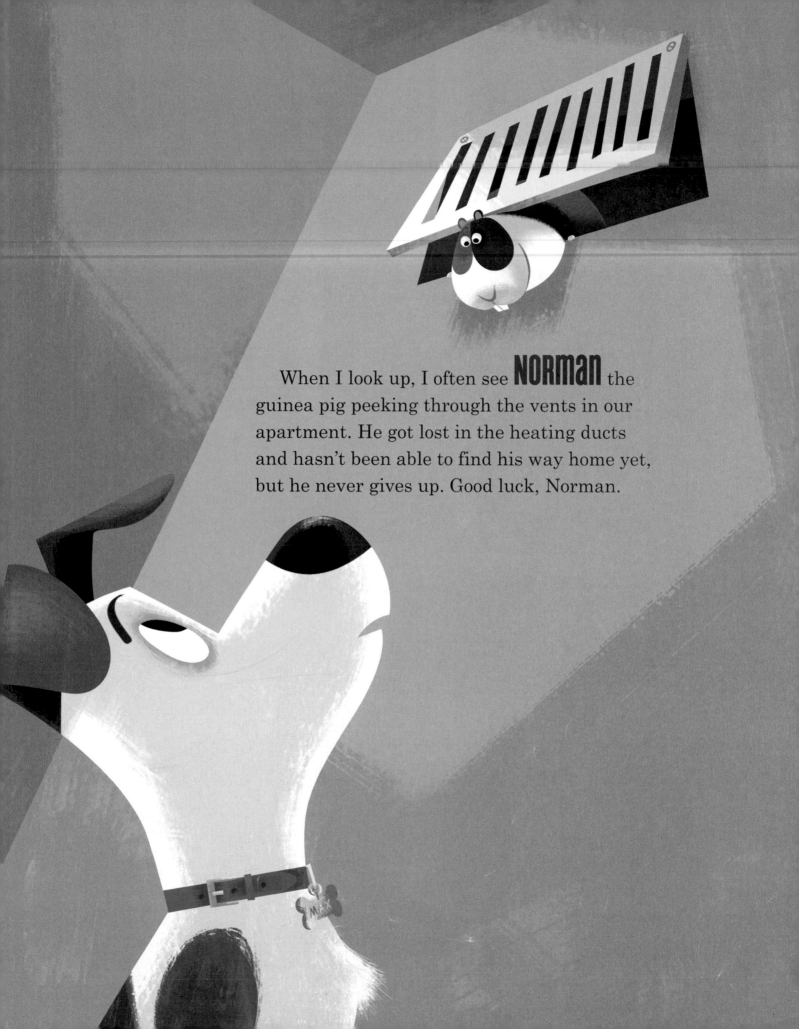

When I look up, I often see **NORMAN** the guinea pig peeking through the vents in our apartment. He got lost in the heating ducts and hasn't been able to find his way home yet, but he never gives up. Good luck, Norman.

And then there's POPS. Since his owner is never home, everyone likes to hang out at his place. It's a real pet hot spot.

Don't worry about Pops's wheels—this old basset hound gets along fine. He's been around so long, he knows everyone in New York.

As you can see, my life is pretty sweet. I get to spend the day with my friends, and then comes my very favorite moment—when Katie returns home and it's just the two of us again. We are a perfect team, with exactly two members, taking on the world together.

Hey, here's Katie now! And she brought me a surprise! That is just like her! She's so great!

It's a . . .

It's a . . .